W9-ARJ-741

First published in Great Britain 1986 by
Hamish Hamilton Children's Books
Garden House, 57–59 Long Acre, London WC2E 9JZ

British Library Cataloguing in Publication Data

Snell, Nigel
A bird in the hand.
I. Title
823'.914[J] PZ7

ISBN 0–241–11815–8

Typeset by Kalligraphics Ltd, Redhill
Printed in Great Britain by
Cambus Litho, East Kilbride

Nigel Snell

A BIRD IN THE HAND..

a child's guide to sayings

Hamish Hamilton · London

People in glass houses shouldn't throw stones.

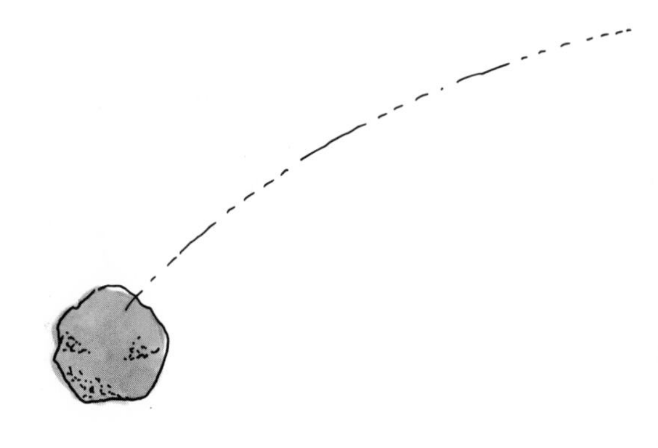

Don't criticise other people unless you are sure they can't criticise you.

It's the last straw that breaks the camel's back.

One extra problem, on top of lots of others, makes them all too heavy to bear.

Don't look a gift horse in the mouth.

If you are given a present, don't examine it for faults. Look pleased and say thank-you.

A bird in the hand is worth two in the bush.

Something you actually have is worth much more than something you only hope to get in the future.

Pride comes before a fall.

Don't imagine you are cleverer than other people because sooner or later you will be proved wrong.

CRASH BANG OUCH CRASH BANG WALLOP OUCH CRASH BANG WALLOP OUCH CRASH
BANG WALLOP OUCH CRASH BANG WALLOP OUCH CRASH BANG WALLOP OUCH CRASH BANG WALLOP OUCH CRASH
CRASH BANG WALLOP OUCH CRASH BANG OUCH CRASH BANG WALLOP
CRASH BANG WALLOP OUCH CRASH BANG WALLOP OUCH CRASH BANG WALLOP CRASH BANG WALLOP CRASH
ROAD UP DANGER!

A rolling stone gathers
no moss.

Someone who is always on the
move never achieves a secure
position in life.

P

Don't count your chickens before they are hatched.

Never think something is yours until it actually belongs to you.

1.
2.
3.
4.
5.
6.
7.
8.
9.
10.

A stitch in time saves nine.

If you do something promptly, you will save time later on.

A new broom sweeps clean.

A new arrival likes to make a fresh start.

SOLD
COUGH
COUGH

There's no smoke without fire.

There's some truth in most stories.

The early bird catches the worm.

People who make an effort get the best out of life.

RING
RING

The proof of the pudding is in the eating.

You can't judge how good something is until you actually try it.

SNELL, NIGEL 02/11/88
A BIRD IN THE HAND
(4) 1986 J398.9 SNE
0652 03 494537 01 3 (IC=1)
B06520349453701 3B

DATE			